Until
KAYLA

LOVING SERIES AND UNTIL SERIES CROSSOVER

CC MONROE

Xoxo CC Monroe

NOTE FROM WORLD CREATOR

Dear Readers,

Welcome to the Happily Ever Alpha Kindle World.

I personally chose each author participating in the Happily Ever Alpha Kindle World because I love their books, and the way they tell a story. That said, this book is entirely the work of the author who wrote it, and I didn't have any part in the process of writing the story.

Enjoy the BOOM!

xoxo Aurora Rose Reynolds

Chapter 1

KAYLA

"I MISS YOU," I WHISPER TO THE HOME I GREW UP IN. IT'S HERE THAT I learned to ride a bike and other childhood milestones. It holds all the beautiful moments that taught me who I was and how to love. But now, it's a symbol of what I lost.

I peer over the two-story home, with green shutters that my parents let me help paint when I was just six, my eyes traveling over the years of wear and tear that made my house a home. I feel the tears stinging my eyes, burning to find an escape, and they nearly do when I look down at the cement of our walkway to the front porch. There I see my tiny handprints between my mother and father's, with *Mackey Family, Best Friends Forever* written permanently below it.

"Mama. Papa." I bring my hand to my heart, and a montage of memories flood my brain, ending with the day they both passed on. That accident tragically took them away, and now I stand alone on the cusp of a new beginning, wishing so badly they were atop those stairs, waving me off with air-blown kisses and beaming smiles.

"They're here and they are so proud," my cousin Kate interrupts my nostalgic memories that aid my broken heart.

Her blonde hair and blue eyes are a contrast from my long brown hair, ending just above my butt, and green eyes with flecks of brown and gold. I give her a meek smile and peer back up. Today, just shy of two years after I lost my parents, I'm leaving the home, where I took time to mourn and lose myself in missing them, to go off to college in Tennessee.

"You think?" I gnaw at the inside of my cheek and do my damnedest to hold off the tears that are really trying to make their pesky way out. I don't like seeming weak, when it's a time I should be happy and strong to most people, over the loss of my parents. But that will never happen. I died inside the night they did. I lost me when I lost them.

College is me following through on my promise to them, but it's now more of an escape, in hopes that I find something to just make me feel again. *God, I want to feel again.*

"You better believe it, Kayla bug," she assures, giving me a tight squeeze into her side.

"Hey, y'all ready? We gotta hit the road if we are gonna make it there by tomorrow!" Sadie, Kate's best friend, hollers from the giant SUV we rented with a small U-Haul attached. We have a long way from my home in Portland to my new apartment in Tennessee. But to say I'm ready to leave behind my home for just a little while—because I didn't sell it—would be a lie. I need a fresh start and new perspective, but it still stings like a bee.

"Come on, bug. It's time for a new start, right?" Kate prompts.

I nod, looking at her just as she brings her forehead to mine, and we share a genuine understanding smile. "Right." And just like that, she leaves me and I look up one more time.

"I'll see you soon. Bye, Mama and Papa."

I make it to the car, and with a heavy heart, I watch my old life in the rearview mirror as I say a silent prayer that my new life will reawaken the old me. The one who used to laugh hard and love even louder. The one who could stay up all night laughing and baking with her mama, and hang with my papa and all the boys. The one who wasn't always lost and looking.

Before they passed, I was always the life of the party, and that came with being an only child. My parents and I spent all our time together, and we all had vivacious personalities that others would cling to. Now, with the exception of Kate and Sadie, my friends started calling less and less, and my life became emptier and emptier.

We all stay silent for a bit, and I know the two of them are letting me simply feel. Sadie—she is the most religious out of all of us, and I know she is probably saying a million prayers a minute in her mind as I sit in the back seat, trying to pick which side of the tug-of-war my heart and brain are playing that I should be on.

Kate and Sadie left behind their rock star lovers to help me move this weekend, and for that, I'm thankful. Because even if inside I'm good at hiding I'm a wreck of emotions, I still couldn't have made this trip alone. Sadie's dominating, obsessive, and strikingly handsome husband is a saint for letting her come, when he usually can't spend a moment away from her. And Kate's boyfriend is probably too high on drugs to even know she is gone. Guess we all have something we are struggling with, and maybe we can find an escape on this trip.

Here's to wishful thinking.

"Y'all, I think we need to have some road trippin' car karaoke!" Sadie breaks up the heavy, and I actually laugh at her sweet southern voice matched with enthusiasm.

"You're on, but if I win, then you get to let me prank call Ben and tease him by telling him you keep getting hit on by random drivers passing by. I always like making that alpha moody!" I chuckle and it feels good. Kate hears it and shoots me a wink, while Sadie just rolls her eyes and turns up the volume.

"Fine! Game on." Then the loud sounds of a Maroon 5 song fill the car, and they start belting it out, lightening the mood and distracting me like I need.

Chapter 2

JASE

I CHECK MYSELF OVER IN THE MIRROR OF MY BATHROOM AND HEAR THE light tapping sounds of my little's feet coming down the hall. "Daddy?" she calls, and like a little beacon of the only light left in my life, she makes me smile as her face appears next to me at the bottom right of the bathroom mirror.

"Yes, princess?" She fell asleep on my chest last night as we watched her favorite *Despicable Me* movie. Avery, my five-year-old pride and joy, is still wearing her princess dress. I swear she would never take it off if I didn't make her. She looks just like her mama as her dimples deepen with my nickname. She has Lainey's eyes, brown with touches of honey running through them.

Every morning, when she wakes up and smiles at me like that, I swear I feel a tight grip in my chest as I remember her mother. My wife died three years ago of ovarian cancer, and it still tears through me like a riptide when I see our daughter look up at me with a smile so big

I would do anything to shield her from the pain.

"You know you're going to have to change before I take you to Nana's, right?" I lift her up in my arms, and her eyes meet mine.

Avery looks deep in my soul when she grasps my jaw, covered in a light five o'clock shadow, in her hands. "No, Daddy. Nana Mae says I can wear this everyday when I see her."

I smile, my dimples now matching hers as her little voice innocently convinces me that my mother is right and I'm wrong. I swear my ma is always pitting her against me. She studies my face, intrigued by my nose, like she has been since she was a baby, pulling and squeezing it. "I think Nana Mae spoils you rotten."

Avery pinches my cheeks and giggles, and that sound makes me puff out my chest. This little ball of light and laughter is my world, and I'm blessed to have her here with me. She makes the hard fucking days bearable.

"No, Daddy, she doesn't. She says you are just a caveman." She chuckles then makes a funny noise, mimicking the sound of a Neanderthal. I make note to tell my mom to stop teaching her how to be my demise. I'm surely fucked. Because when Avery grows up, I will have to buy a shotgun for every room, so I have easy access to one when any fucker tries to get in to date my daughter. Just that thought has me angry inside and out, my body going hot.

"'No, Daddy. No, Daddy.' What am I going to do with you, little bug?" I start tickling her, and she struggles to break free while thrashing in a fit of laughter.

"You will just have to give me to Nana! She'll protect

me!" she yells around a hard laugh from deep in her gut.

"Not possible, little one. I'm your protector." I stop tickling, and her laughs settle as she catches her breath. "And my protector you will always be," she whispers back to me what I taught her to always respond with when I say that. That was the first daddy/daughter lesson I taught her when she really started to talk. It's the words of my soul, and I hope she never loses sight of that, even when she finds someone and no longer puts me first. I even have the words tattooed on my chest, so I take her everywhere with me.

I immediately shove that thought to the back of my mind so I don't lose my shit in the bathroom before work. Setting her on her feet, I tell her, "Go get your bag ready. We're gonna be late, and Nana said she's making you pancakes."

"Pancakes!" she hollers, running back to her room down the hall, our moment long forgotten by a child's attention span.

Turning back, I take another look at myself and decide it will do. My hair is in desperate need of a cut, and today I did my best to style it. *That will have to fucking do,* I think to myself as I leave the bathroom. Today I have a busy day ahead, meeting with contractors for the new housing development going up on the outskirts of town. I do home design blueprints, and I'm meeting with the investors to show them the four different home designs we plan to build on the land.

I run my own business from home most the time, but every once in a while, especially in the start of construction, I'm the busiest. I make great money, and I get to spend time with Avery more than most parents do.

"All right, little one. Let's go," I holler from the front door, and seconds later, she comes bounding down the hall and into the front room. Still in her princess dress, she went with tennis shoes, and her hair is a mess.

I can't send her to my mom's this way; she will throw a fit. These are the moments I realize my lack of dating life is killing me. I can't do her hair in ways a mother can, or nurture her in a way a woman can. I'm afraid she is going to grow up resentful if one day I don't give her a mother to help her grow into the young woman I know she will one day want to be.

But no one has ever been able to spark a need in me. I haven't touched another woman since Lainey passed, and the one date I went on ended in disaster when my best man, Harlen, thought dating a hooker would help.

That smug fucker is always doing shit to pull my chain. That reminds me; I'm supposed to meet him and his girl tonight.

"Come here, crazy girl." I scoop her up and walk back toward the bathroom, setting her on the counter as she smiles up at me, unfazed. She was too young when her mom died, and that is the only thing I can find comfort in. Because if Avery ever had the chance to know how incredible Lainey was, her mourning would've been unbearable.

I find her brush and start untangling the knots as gently as my six-foot, bulky frame can. My hands alone are bigger than her face. I always fear I'm going to hurt her, but she's tough. The makings of a girl raised by her father.

"What are you smiling and giggling about, chuckles?" I smile down at her when I take note of her light laughter.

"You should see your face, Daddy. You look so scared." Her tiny hands come to her lips, and she laughs when I furrow my brow.

"I'm not scared. This is my normal face."

"That's not a good one." She shakes her head, still smiling.

"Are you saying I'm not good-looking?" I act affronted, teasing her. Nodding her head, her smile deepens. "Oh that's it, little bug. Come here!" I finish her hair, and then pick her up over my shoulder, wrapping my arms extra tight around her legs so she doesn't slip.

"Daddy! Put me down!" She wiggles and squirms, but her laughter tells me she loves every second. I know I am. My only light—she is my only light.

"Nope, we are dropping you off at Nana's just like this!" I bring my hand to her sides, just next to my head, and I tickle her.

She fights some more until I swoop up her bag and get us out the door. Once in the car, she sits in the back seat, singing and talking nonstop about her plans with Nana for the day.

This is my life, just the two of us.

Chapter 3

KAYLA

"MY ASS IS LIKE A ROCK. I THINK I NEED A GOOD MASSAGE. SADIE, YOU feel like squeezing up on this," Kate teases, as we all climb out of the SUV we have spent the past two days in. We all laugh, and Sadie rolls her eyes, used to Kate's harassing.

"I'm good. We shared a bed last night, and I think you grabbed my boob three times in your sleep," Sadie responds as I move to the back of the U-Haul to open it up and retrieve my things. We pulled up outside the tiny house I'm renting just a few blocks away from the university, and it's just as small and quaint as the pictures made it seem.

All white with yellow shutters. There isn't a ton of people surrounding me, just one neighbor a mile down the road, and then another about five hundred yards from me. The two-bedroom one-bathroom 1920s home is just right for little ole me.

"You liked it, Sister Christian. Don't lie," Kate retorts, as they both approach me.

"Shut it, weirdo."

"Both of you hush and help me. I have a mini U-Haul to unpack and you are slowing us down." They both jump to attention and we share smiles.

"Lead the way, sir." Kate salutes. I go to say something back, planning to get in the last word, when the roar of a motorcycle stops me.

"Hey, do y'all need help?" a beautiful woman with curly hair asks from behind the biker's shoulder. He has dark hair and a thick beard. It's like looking at night and day, hard and soft. Instantly, you can tell they're a couple when he places his hand possessively on her hip after she climbs off the bike. He doesn't say anything, but his eyes stay glued to her, as if we are going to turn into kidnappers and take her away. It's wildly scary, but recklessly hot. What I wouldn't give for a man to protect me fiercely like him.

"Oh no, that's okay! We don't want to put anyone out," I respond with a soft smile.

"Babe, you aren't in Portland anymore," she points to the plates on our vehicle. "We help our neighbors out around here. Right, handsome?" She looks over her shoulder at the stoic beast behind her, and with that, he stands. I think we all gulp when he towers over her, pulling her into his side as he does.

The man is big. A real biker. Leather cut and all. And suddenly, I'm the nervous one.

"Whatever my woman wants, she gets. So where does what go, ladies?" His demeanor throws me off a bit. He looks too big to be so nice and welcoming. There is a gentle giant vibe about him, and we all notice.

She starts, "Harmony MacCabe. And this big teddy—" and he growls, my stomach filling with butterflies. Holy moly, he is gorgeous. "—is my caveman husband, Harlen, and we are here to help you."

"Wow, that really is sweet of you. My name's Kayla, and this is my cousin, Kate, and her babysitter, Sadie," I tease, and Kate nudges my side.

"Hey! I'm a hoot. You are going to miss me when we leave," she says with a pout before crossing her arms.

"Wait, you're the only one living here? As in, alone? No husband or roommates?" Harlen asks, his brows drawing in with his scowl.

"Um, no, I-I just..." I stutter suddenly, intimidated by his dominance.

"Oh hush. Not all of us women are damsels. We can live on our own, Harlen. Remember? I did." Harmony rolls her eyes and leaves his side.

"I know that, baby. But still, she's new in town, and she doesn't have many neighbors."

"I taught her how to royally screw up someone's balls if they come at her, so no worries." Kate shrugs next to me, and while all the girls chuckle, Harlen stays stone-faced.

"Ignore him. Brooding and all-alpha. That's my big man."

I do what Harmony says and make work of unpacking. Within two hours, everything is in the house and some of the boxes are open.

"Thank you, guys. You made this go by way faster," I tell Harmony and Harlen.

"Oh, no problem. Welcome to town." She eyes me

over, Kate and Sadie lost in the mix of boxes down the hall in my room. "Hey, how about y'all come out with us tonight? We're getting together at the local joint with some friends."

"Really? I mean, you don't have to invite me. I don't want to impose."

"You sure say that a lot. Listen, I like you. You're quiet, and I wouldn't invite you if I didn't dig your vibe, lady."

I smile shyly, tucking my hair awkwardly, because I'm not used to this much social interaction. I've kept so much to myself for the past two and half years that I've lost my natural flare for socializing.

"I like you too, both of you. Except, *you* kind of scare me." Before I can stop it, those words fly out of my mouth, and I cover it as my eyes go to the man I was speaking about, Harlen. Everyone goes silent, and I'm sure my invite is about to be retracted.

When Harmony finally snorts, trying to hold in her laughter, Harlen cracks a crooked grin, and my shoulders relax a little.

"I'll take it. It's the beard and the muscles. Makes most people scared. Except this one. It turns her on. Can't keep her off me." His hand on her hip turns her into him, and he gives her butt a full-on squeeze, setting off those tiny shivers in my belly again. Wow. He uses his free hand as she starts to protest his comment, when he grips her jaw and slams his mouth to hers. I watch her sag in his arms and become putty in his hands.

"Ah, that effect. Ben still gets me like that too," Sadie says, as she and Kate reenter the room. I look to her and shake my head with wide eyes.

"You are very lucky then. That isn't something you see in men these days," Kate tells her, while Sadie and I keep our eyes on the show.

Finally, Harmony breaks up their PG-13/borderline R-rated make-out scene. "So sorry. He's a caveman."

He wipes his lip with his thumb and smacks her on the ass, turning to step outside. Grumbling over his shoulder something along the lines of her loving it.

"Are all his friends like that?" I tease, but her body perks up, her eyes going wild with an idea. I gulp, because I feel like something crazy is about to happen, a twist in my gut telling me a hand of fate is about to knock me square on my ass.

"Yeah, they are. In fact, Jase, Harlen's good friend since childhood, is gonna be there tonight. I think you two would hit it off!" She jumps on the balls of her feet and bites her bottom lip.

"Baby, don't you go meddling again." Harlen steps into the house with a box we must have missed.

"Hush, I'm not meddling. I'm simply directing traffic."

My brows pull in, and I watch their exchange, still trying to figure out what is happening. Jase? Meddling? We would hit it off? Why is my stomach a mess of anxious butterflies, but my mind is screaming to run and hide and fake the flu to get out of tonight?

"He's gonna be pissed, and then I'm gonna have to kick his ass if he gets snippy with you. You're playing with fire, baby."

"This sounds promising," I mumble.

"We will be there!" Kate interjects, making the decision, and there is no way she will let me out of this now. Kate and Harmony could be soul sisters.

I grow more and more anxious. I haven't been with a guy, not since my short high school fling with Joey. It was nothing, just two awkward teens making out in the back seat of a car. Hands always to ourselves. How would I even act or talk to a man if he's anything like Harmony's alpha giant?

"Perfect, what's your number?" She pulls out her phone, and I rattle off my number nervously. Seconds later, I have a text with the place and time. "There. I'm so excited! Let's head home, Harlen. I have to shower and get ready. We will see you ladies tonight!" Harmony comes in for a hug and I return it, still a mess over everything that's transpired. Who am I right now? How did I not even argue with all of them? It's like the universe is pulling and clawing at me to follow Harmony in the direction she's pointing me.

"Yeah, we will see you there," I say timidly, letting the war rage on in my mind.

Calm down, Kayla. It's just a group activity, not your damn wedding day. I shake it off and finish with goodbyes. Now, to find the box where I packed my decent clothing. Can't go in ripped sweat pants and my dad's tee.

Mama and Papa. I remember them then, and I remember why I came here. New beginnings. New things. Tonight will be the start.

Chapter 4

JASE

"HOLD ON A SECOND. HARMONY." I DRAG OUT HER NAME AND GLARE AT her sweet, smirking face in the rearview mirror of my truck.

"What?" she responds innocently, as if she didn't just throw this surprise date on me while we're on our way.

"Easy, Riding. I've been kicking ass since we were young. Don't come at my lady."

I give Harlen a sideways incredulous look.

Harmony tries to warm the sudden chill in the air. "Listen, it's not a date. I just invited her along."

I'm not letting her off the hook that easy. I know her better then she thinks I do. I haven't found one woman to light a spark in my chest—or as Harmony puts it, I haven't found my "boom"—and I don't think that will change anytime soon. It's not that I'm opposed to finding love. I just can't seem to connect inside with anyone in the way I need it. I'm a father, I'm a business man, I'm a grown adult, and I no longer chase pussy. My soul is

CC MONROE

fucking looking for his match, and he can't find her. Now, who knows who this stranger is Harmony met today? She may be an emotional nightmare who gets attached, and when I'm not interested, she might snap.

"You think you're sly?" I ask.

She leans forward, wrapping her arms around my shoulders and getting as close to my ear as she can from her seat belt's restriction. "Just trust me, big guy. She's sweet, and who knows? Maybe it's a chance to simply make another friend." I smile and shake my head, taking this chance. She pokes my dimple. "There's that handsome smile."

"All right, baby. You're cut off," Harlen growls, his possessive side rearing its head, and I watch them. He grabs her hand away from me and brings it to his lips for a bite. She squeals, and they get lost in their cheesy love bubble.

I had love with Lainey, but never anything like that. We had affection and sex, but not possession and passion. She was my high school sweetheart, and I loved her with everything in me. I would be happily married still, but that kind of connection, that palpable I-would-die-for-you kind of love, we didn't reach that. I most likely never will, because I believe Harlen is just a head case. I mean, I can just breathe in Harmony's direction, and he's ready to maul me. Don't even get me started on how he reacts to anyone who isn't in his close circle. A biker who packs is not a man you want to fuck with, especially if it involves his lady.

"I already told her not to meddle, man. Can't stop this one when she is up to something," Harlen says nonchalantly.

I give a grunt and pull up to the bar. It's a local joint, and tonight it's not as busy as it usually is for a Friday night. I park and get out, already ready to call it a night. I'm not ready to see any one, especially a woman I don't know who is in God knows what mental state. Shit.

"This way." Harmony heads toward the back, leading us as I follow behind Harlen and her.

"Ladies! Hey!" she greets the group of women, and all I can see from my place behind Harlen is two beautiful blondes.

"Girls, you have already met Harlen. This fella here is Jase, Harlen's friend." I smile at them, and the one with freckles on her nose goes wide-eyed, as the other with a simple gold cross around her neck smiles. They both look up to something. "This is Sadie and Kate. Oh, and Harlen, step aside so Jase can meet Kayla."

With that, she moves, and I swear to fuck, my heart stammers in my chest, nearly stopping at the sight in front of me. "Fuck."

"Wow," she says at the same time.

Kayla is breathtaking. Long brown hair with blonde tips. Green eyes that look like a gypsy's, surrounded by dark lashes. Her body calls to me like a siren. Curvy, toned, and tight, sculpted by gods from what I see. I'm stuck in place, my muscles tense and accumulating heat. And I know our meeting hit her too, because the music around us has drowned out and we are locked in an intense stare-off that neither of us can break.

"I'm—wow, this is embarrassing. I'm Kayla," she speaks first, and I cough. Clearing the frog in my fucking throat.

I look like a complete moron.

"Kayla, I'm Jase. It's nice to meet you." I touch her hand, and once again, something sparks. I swear she shocks me with her presence.

"Wow, the last time I saw a man look at a woman like that is the day Ben Cooper spotted you from the stage, Sadie Jay," the blonde named Kate says.

"Yeah. Her reaction is about the same as mine," Sadie whispers back.

"Man." Harlen pats my back with a heavy hand, and I do my best to get my shit together. But little does everyone else in this damn room know that I just fell face-first into this beautiful woman's depths, and I don't know what the fuck is happening. I have never reacted to a woman this way before. Not even Lainey.

"Let's take a seat and order us some drinks," Harmony chimes in, and Kayla finally breaks eye contact, tucking her curled hair behind those small, dainty ears I would give anything to bite and growl into while she rides me.

Shit. There it is. I don't even know this woman, and I'm already picturing myself inside her. Owning her. Possessing her. Claiming her fucking soul.

We sit, and without planning to, I end up next to her, her body melting into mine. She doesn't look like the type to just give it up or do this very often, and neither am I, but there is a pull there, and we both can't resist it. Crazy part is, we haven't even said more than a sentence or two to each another.

We order drinks. I get myself a Bud Light, and she orders herself a Coke. Once the waitress takes off to collect our drinks and the next bar patron starts singing karaoke on stage, everyone at our table stays focused on the drunk idiot making a fool of himself. But Kayla's eyes keep meeting mine, and I put my arm around her, resting my hand against the plush pleather of the booth behind her.

Leaning in, I bring my lips to her exposed ear. "Who are you." It's more of a proclamation than a question, because she has done something to me. Hypnotized me with her gypsy eyes. And I need to know how to break the fucking trance.

I can't stop my other hand as it travels across my lap and onto her smooth, exposed arm. The little black simple dress is showing off her body in the best way possible, and my hands ache to touch her. I rub the back of my fingers up her arm, and she leans in to whisper back.

"Same to you. I'm not this kind of girl." Kayla's response doesn't shock me. I know she's never been touched by a man in the way she is dying for me to touch her. I can feel it, smell it, fucking taste it in the air.

"You feel it. Don't you?" I question, bringing my lips to the underside of her ear and leaving an open-mouthed kiss. What in the actual fuck am I doing? I have never desired a woman like this, especially without even knowing anything about her. I've never felt so familiar with a total stranger.

"I shouldn't. I don't know if you are a serial killer or just an average Joe." She shivers as my tongue touches her skin. I get a taste of her cherry-scented skin and I growl.

Laughing in my chest at her comment, I remark, "Baby, I'm neither." I'm not an average Joe, especially in her presence. Instead, I'm a man unhinged and wildly untamable. Kayla is awakening something in me, and that scares the shit out of us both. And she doesn't even know it yet.

"If you are neither, then what are you?" She peers up through those thick lashes.

I respond instantly, "Why don't you let me show you? Let's get out of here." I watch the uncertainty flash in her eyes as she wavers on what to do. At least one of us is thinking logically, because all I care about is getting her under me and sliding inside her. Inside her body, inside her mind, and inside wherever the hell she will let me. Because I need answers. So many fucking answers.

Chapter 5

KAYLA

I DON'T KNOW WHAT'S COME OVER ME, BUT I'M SUCKED INTO SOME KIND of trance, and Jase is the hypnotist. He's handsome, breathtaking, the knock-you-on-your-butt, almost surreal type of handsome. And I know he is drawn to me just the same by the way he can't stop looking at me like I'm the center of the room. His rough, calloused hand glides up and down my arm, and his husky, deep voice turns to gravel in my ear as he whispers for us to leave. And though my mouth opens to say no, my heart has other plans.

"Yes." A three-letter word with the promise of unknown seconds, minutes, or hours ahead of me. I don't know Jase. We haven't even established a baseline for conversation. Yet here I am, ready to speak no words and only do whatever he leads me to do.

I've never had a one-night stand, but I'm sure this isn't how they usually go. There isn't just lust behind our glazed eyes. There is a deep urgency to connect, to talk, to chase this feeling until we catch it tightly in our shaking hands.

"Kate, Sadie, um... I'm gonna take off with Jase. Harmony, Harlen, thanks for inviting me." I'm red in the face, flushed over the fact that everyone at this table is giving us a knowing glance.

"Boom," Harmony mouths to me before my eyes drift to Kate and Sadie's, who nod encouragingly.

"Oh no, Sadie Jay, she may be the next you. That Ben Cooper effect is real," Kate says, referring to Sadie and her husband, the rock star she married in less than a month of knowing him. I don't think this will be more than a one-night fling, where I will then spend the next few decades comparing every man to the one who got away.

Jase. He is that man. The one you never see coming and never—*ever*—want to forget.

I don't know what is going to happen the second we step out the bar door, but I can only hope it will be that something I was looking for to make me forget the pain of the past two years. I pray it's going to be the start of a new life, one where I will live each day in the light and not the shadows of my past.

"Where do you live?" He finally speaks when he starts up his truck. The question isn't the first one I expected him to ask. Is he used to this? Am I this kind of girl? One who sleeps with a total stranger who only knows my address before he gets inside me?

"I... I live up Parks Road, just two blocks f-from the university," I stammer out, trepidation obvious in each word.

He says something then that almost frightens me

more than the idea of finally punching my V-card. "Don't be nervous, Kayla. I only want to get to know you."

My eyes find his, sparking as he gets on the main road. It's brief, because he has to focus on driving, but I can't believe he just said that.

"So we aren't going to… you know… have sex?" I about slap my open palm to my forehead, not believing I actually said that out loud.

"No, I don't just fuck women I want to respect, but don't worry." He pauses, reaching over to put his hand on my knee, and instantly, I feel a spark that nearly singes my spine in two. He looks at me with a penetrating gaze, and it's as if I can feel him inside me already. I almost crumble under that intense look. "When I get to know you, you and I won't be able to keep our fucking hands off each other."

I gulp, so loud I'm sure he hears it. "Wow."

"Yeah, it's a first for me too, baby," he says knowingly.

I know he and I are feeling that pull, but I guess we both can't believe just how strong that tug is. We fall silent, and I grow more nervous by the second, lost and unsure what to say.

"So, Harmony told me you moved here from Portland." He speaks first, and the question is easy enough. I can do this.

"Yes, my mom went to college here. I did it to be closer to her." I look down and feel that pang in my chest. *Do not cry.* My fingernails dig into my palms, and I look at the promise ring my mother gave me as a talisman, centering me.

"That's a far way from home. Wouldn't it have been

easier to just stay physically close?"

I close my eyes, knowing this is going to be awkward. "Uh, no. You see, m-my parents passed away two years ago." The slice of regret smells bitter in his truck.

He drops his head and shakes it, letting out a deep breath. "Wow. I'm an idiot. Sorry, baby." He calls me baby as if he's been doing it for years, and in that instant, it feels like he has.

"Do not say sorry. It's not something I announce off the bat, and how would you know?" I reach over and squeeze his hand, comforting him while my heart whirls in pain. I cannot and will not break in front of him. I mean, this is already an unlikely scenario, and I don't want to add me breaking down to the mix. That would be a story for my kids one day.

"What are you going to school for?" Jase asks after we turn off the highway and head toward my place.

"Elementary education, even though I'm sure I will suck at it. I love children, but I don't think they like me. I swear I repel most kids. For instance: Sadie's. She's got a sweet little daughter, and whenever I hold her, she wiggles until she's free. I'm starting to think I have a weird face or maybe I just smell funny." I instantly blush as he laughs deep from his belly, his hand tightening on my thigh.

Nice, Kayla. Talk about having body odor. That will get his rocket shooting.

"I doubt it. Depends on her age. My daughter went through a stage last year where she didn't want anyone to hug her, pick her up, or slow her down. She had to be going all the time."

A daughter? Jase has a daughter. Obviously, he isn't

married, or at least I would hope he's not, since we keep touching one another and he keeps referring to me as baby.

"You have a little girl?"

"Yeah, I do. Her name is Avery. She's five." He pulls down the visor above him and takes out a picture. "She's incredible, way too smart, and keeps me a nervous wreck every damn second of the day." His eyes sparkle when he talks about her, and it's his most breathtaking look yet.

He hands the picture to me, and the little girl smiling through the photo is adorable. Her hair is a wild mess of brown locks, her eyes a similar color to her hair, and her smile is huge as she squeezes a doll to her chest. I can see it on the printed gloss photo that she is most likely the sweetest thing ever. I don't doubt she would send Jase into cardiac arrest multiple times a day.

"She's adorable." I smile over at him, and with one more glance at the picture, I hand it back.

"Avery is adorable, but she is a handful. Ask my fucking cardiologist," he jokes, and it lightens the mood again. I make note to ask him about her mother at a later time. We already touched on some deep stuff, and I don't want this moment to pass.

"Poor thing. Oh, my house is that one right there." I point to the little white house with a porch light on just up the road.

"There's no one around you. You have roommates?" He parks, and we both unbuckle.

"Nope, just me." I watch his nose flare, and his eyes bore into the house like it's reached out and slapped him.

"What is it?"

"It's not safe to live out here all alone, baby," he says, his voice stern.

"That's exactly what your friend Harlen said, except he was way scarier. That man is huge. And it's fine. I'm not a damsel in distress. I know how to kick someone's ass if need be, *baby*."

His eyes find mine and he looks shocked. "You making fun of the way I call you baby?"

I smirk and open the truck to jump out. I'm feeling lightheaded and playful and so unbelievably comfortable in this man's presence. Turning back on him fast, his face still locked in shock, I wink. "Maybe I am. Or maybe I just like calling *you* baby." I slam the door and start heading up the walkway, biting my lip in complete and utter disbelief. I haven't been this carefree or bold since years ago.

"You little fucking minx." I'm shocked and yelp when I'm suddenly looking at the backside of Jase and his perfect Levi-encased ass. Holy hell. I didn't even hear him coming up behind me. How did he throw me over his shoulder so damn fast?

"Ahh! Jase! I'm wearing a dress!" I try to reach back to cover my lady parts that I'm sure are out for him to see. I'm thankful I don't have neighbors close enough to get a look out their window.

"I know, and damn that lace for having the great fucking honor of covering that peach."

I gasp when I feel a sharp sensation on my upper thigh closest to his face. "Did you just bite me?" I ask, astonished yet excited, my core tightening with my question—completely betraying me.

"Sure did, sassy little thing. You asked for it," he

rumbles. I have an idea, and it hits me fast. Before I can stop myself, I go for it. "Hey! Oh, you fucking tease." He sets me on my feet and looks back to where his hand is rubbing his ass before turning back to me with a cocky, playful grin. "Did you just bite my ass?"

"Sure did," I remark, mimicking the same tone he used on me. "You brought it on yourself." I run up the stairs then to my door and try to unlock the door with shaking hands. Jase is on me then, his front clinging to my back, his tall frame looming over me. He slides one hand up the side of my thigh, up under my dress, and leaves it firmly gripping my hip, where the lace of my panties sits. His lips find my neck, and his hot tongue begins to travel all around my weak spots. This is happening. I know it.

Once the key finally works, the door swings open and he has me against the wall of my small foyer. Lifting me up and around him with little effort, he thrusts forward and lets his hips hold me up. I feel his cock straining against his jeans, and I whimper into his mouth, our tongues fighting and taking more and more with each second, and even then, we can't get enough.

"Jase," I moan his name, and it feels familiar. Why? I don't know. But in this moment, I decide to stop second-guessing it or asking myself questions. I want to feel this moment, even if this is what it will only ever be—a fleeting moment that will be chased away by the morning sun.

"Say you're okay with this and that you want me, baby." He finally gives us room to breathe. Our foreheads touch, and his eyes stay shut as if he is trying to mentally talk himself down. I taste the mint from his tongue on mine, and smell his natural manly scent, making me crumble as it breezes across my face.

"I want you to be my first," I whisper, kissing just his top lip.

"What? This is your first time?" His eyes are open and his breathing has evened out.

I nod, biting my lip, my eyes watering from the real, raw desire consuming my body. I can't even find the words.

"Don't answer me with lust. Answer me with words and feelings, baby." He leans in and kisses my cheek, then my forehead and the tip of my nose.

"I want you tonight, Jase. I want you to be the first man to touch my body."

"Fuck." Just like that, he places me back on my feet, and I would stumble, but he keeps a firm grasp on me.

"Undress, beautiful. Slide off your dress and show me your perfect skin."

I stand nervously, his hands still on my hips as I process what he just asked me to do. "It's not perfect."

"I doubt that. Because everything else about you has been perfect so far."

Nearly purring and blushing like a praised fool, I melt into him. I don't need to second-guess myself. Jase will make me a woman tonight, and if this is the only time we ever touch or talk again, it won't make me regret this night.

I reach down, and with one swoop, I remove my dress and he gulps, his eyes glazing over as he stands back. With one hand, he reaches out to touch my hipbone. My chest is bare, being that my breasts are small yet enough and perky, so I don't have to have a bra.

"Your panties, I want to take them off myself, beautiful. Is that okay?" Jase is soft with not only his touches but his words, and I feel that much safer.

"You don't have to ask. I'm yours tonight, Jase."

"You think tonight will only be tonight, and you are wrong, Kayla. Tonight is just the fucking beginning. You're mine."

I'm completely robbed of words. Holy hell, that feeling I desired when Harlen spoke to Harmony the way he did comes to life. I have heard men like Harlen and Ben talk to their women this way, but never did I believe I would be under the spell of a man who would speak that way to me. And now that I am, I know I will never be able to go without it.

The delicate feeling of his calloused fingertips makes me shiver as he slides my panties from my body. On his haunches, I become aware of his nearness, and no man has ever been this close to me before. I'm nervous Jase will be disappointed in what he sees. I don't wax, I just trim, and I'm sure the women this man has been with are perfectly groomed. Jase is older than I am, so he's probably had his fair share of women. That doesn't still my frantic heart, so I push it aside and pray he takes me for what I am.

I peer down, risking a look to see what his reaction to me is, and I'm nearly knocked back into the wall, more than I already am.

"Fucking beautiful. Breathtaking. Perfect—I knew you would be perfect, baby." Looking up from under his thick lashes, his head comes in closer to my core, and before I can question him, he kisses my pubic bone then nips it before soothing it with an open-mouthed kiss.

I bend at the waist and let out a whimper before jolting back into the wall, my hand grabbing a fistful of his hair. "Shit." A slip of the tongue, unable to handle the sensation.

"Bedroom, point," he demands, kissing my slit, and the arousal deepens in the pit of my stomach as I nearly combust.

Standing when I follow through, he lifts me up again, my legs banding around his waist. I wrap my arms around his neck, and we share lazy, slow kisses, the kind you give someone you've known as a lover for years. That's how real this feels, how unbelievably natural this connection seems to be.

"You taste like something I've been missing," he whispers against my lips as he leads me into my bedroom, where boxes line the wall and the only thing put together is my nightstand and bed. Thank God for Sadie and Kate's help today, or we would be making love on hardwood floor.

"What have you been missing?" I whisper when he lays me gently on the bed and stands back to remove his shirt. I watch the muscles bunch, move, and tighten on his six-pack as he removes the material, and my mouth goes completely dry. I have never seen such perfection; he's built like a god, like the men you see in movies and fantasize about—but better. One hundred times better.

"A fucking heartbeat."

I melt under his words. Who is this man, and what is his story? Because I think he may be just as broken as I am.

"I couldn't find mine either, until tonight. You made it beat again," I confess. He should feel like a stranger, but instead he is on the cusp of being so much more.

Now fully naked, with lust and promise in our eyes, he climbs onto the bed, his hard cock intimidating me.

"It's going to hurt, beautiful, but I promise to be slow and gentle with you."

I nod nervously, with rapid jerks of my head. "Okay."

He smiles gently, crawling over me, using his elbows to hold his body weight as one hand cradles my face. I swallow thickly past the nerves in my throat, and we lock in a heated gaze. "You ready?"

"I am."

"Are you on the pill?" he asks, reaching down between us and finding my clit. I cry out, the sensation overwhelming. He may be only touching my clit, but it feels like he is touching everywhere, as if he's in every cell of my body.

"Y-yes," I stutter, my hands gripping the sheet as he picks up speed. It's then I feel something enticing growing in my belly, a slow burn that boils to the surface.

"Good, now come for me, beautiful. Let go."

I do on command. "Oh my God, Jase! Stop! It's... its too much!" I try and climb away as my orgasm jolts me nearly off the bed. I'm running from the incredible sensation, while trying my damnedest to get closer to it.

"Fuck, baby, I can't wait. I need you," he growls, and before I can settle, I feel his cock at my entrance, collecting my juices as he prepares to take me. "Look me in the eyes. Tell me if it's too much, okay?"

"I will, baby."

"I love it when you call me that." He smiles through his response, and it's the perfect moment to join us together for a night I will never forget, and pray it will not be the last.

Biting my lip as the first inch goes in, I'm completely aware of ever nerve-ending in my body. He goes slowly, giving me inch by inch with a kiss to my lips.

"Let it out, baby. This is going to hurt." He walks me through it, and with one more thrust, he breaks through and I cry out.

No longer a virgin and now a woman. His woman.

"Jase!"

"So fucking perfect and tight. My girl."

"Presumptuous," I squeak, trying to distract myself from the pain.

"Call it that if you will, but the moment I broke that barrier and claimed your body, you became mine. And I don't share, Kayla."

I'm suddenly gasping for air, waiting for this dream to end. "We will see what the morning brings us," I try to brush it off, not wanting to get my hopes up where they shouldn't be.

"I already know. You'll be riding my face as I make you mine indefinitely."

My core clenches, and the pain starts to disappear. Holy hell, I never knew dirty talk could call to the deepest parts of me.

"There it is. You like that idea too, baby, and I know this shit didn't happen for no reason." He picks up his pace, and I know I won't be able to last long.

"Then why don't you take me like you own me?"

"Letting a stranger own you. If I wasn't that stranger, I would spank you for giving your body to one." He moves, sitting up on his knees and gripping my hips. The new position has him deeper inside me.

"Maybe I want you to spank me," I tease, my head rolling back when he strokes my clit. "Ahh!"

"Next time. Right now, I'm making love to you. It's your first time, beautiful."

"Such a gentleman," I moan, reaching up to grab my hair, and I can't help but notice the emboldened words slip out of me so easily, the way they used to years ago.

He doesn't miss a beat, pounding inside me. "No, baby, I'm an alpha. Big fucking difference. Now come for me again. Come with me." I watch him bite his lip and I mimic it. Totally enthralled. In this moment, I'm his and he is mine. "Don't you dare stop. Come on, give me one. Chase that feeling." I do what he says, and I let my body be owned as I let myself feel him deep. Forgetting everything then, I feel him expand inside me. "Pretty baby, come for me." He pinches my nipples, taking nearly my entire breast in his hand as I come hard. This time, it's more intense, my core clenching tightly around his shaft.

"Fuck. Damn it." He comes then, growling my name, the vein in his neck protruding as he keeps up the steady pace.

"Jase!" I grip his hand on my chest and ride out the waves. His come fills me, and it solidifies our connection and this night.

I gave my body to Jase, and I know now that if I'm not careful, he might steal my heart.

Chapter 6

JASE

THE MORNING SUN SHINES IN FROM THE WINDOW, AND THE SOUND OF two low voices coming from down the hall has me waking against my will. Usually when you wake up in a foreign place, you have a lapse in memory, but not me—not this time anyway. Last night, I made love to Kayla, claimed her innocence, and got myself into deep water that I can't surface from now. When Harmony told me she invited someone for me to meet, I didn't think that someone would make me feel anything last night, but she did. Kayla and her mesmerizing eyes and sweet, innocent way lit a torch in my once dark, empty heart.

I haven't felt this since before Lainey died. At the same time it warms me, it also makes me feel guilty. I never thought I could feel again, because Lainey deserved all my love—she was beyond perfection, and I was unworthy of her. Now, after barely getting to know each other, I have slept with an angel, and she has claimed something in me. What it is, I'm not sure yet. But does that mean

Lainey is so easily replaceable?

No. I feel her here now, inside my heart, tearing apart the walls I built after her death and begging me to let someone else in. To feel again. I have to trust in her, because she never let me down; she never steered me wrong. In this moment, I choose to play this out, to let it consume me and hope for the fucking best.

I hear who I'm sure are Kayla's girlfriends whispering in the kitchen, but I don't listen in too closely. I'm more than a hundred percent sure they are talking about us. Shit, half of this part of Tennessee probably is.

I lie flat on my back and tilt my head down, taking in the beauty lost in slumber next to me. Fuck, she is beautiful. Lying on the soft, plush skin of her stomach, the curve of her spine is catching most of the morning sun. The side of her breast is playing peekaboo as it presses to my side. Her hand rests comfortably on my chest. Her hair covers the pillow on the other side of her, her makeup wiped away from hours of rolling around in bed and heated touches.

I see her in a different light, a better light—a more captivating one. Her lips pout, and it seems the sound of her soft breathing echoes in the room, bringing me all the way into her space. I'm consumed.

My ma used to say that you will find real love and true beauty in the early morning light, when an angel lies beside you and steals your very soul. And in this moment, I know I was stolen, and I know I'm completely fucked.

I want to wake her with my cock inside her snug heat, with me so deep inside she can feel me with each inhale and exhale. Climbing out of bed as smoothly as I can, making sure not to wake her, I move to the bedroom door and shut it, giving us some privacy. Turning to return to bed, Kayla is sitting up, the sheets pulled up close to her chest.

"Hi," she whispers nervously.

"Good morning, gorgeous." She eyes me up and down, taking in my completely naked body. I try not to smirk cockily, because I see she is really admiring me in a new way, the same way I did to her just minutes ago.

"You're still here?" She tucks her hair behind her ear, finally letting her eyes leave me. She's so nervous, and it's both worrisome and adorable.

"I am, yes, and I plan to be here until I have to go meet Harlen in an hour." I would call and cancel, but I promised him I would help him build and move furniture. Avery is still asleep, I'm sure, because Saturdays with my mom always means she sleeps in, so that gives me time before I have to give her our morning call.

"Oh, I just thought that you would be gone." She peers up at me, those green eyes glistening.

"If this was a one-night stand, I would have been."

"Isn't it?" she questions, and I don't like it. Grabbing the sheet at the end of the bed, I give it a brisk, effortless tug as she tries to save it from leaving her body. She's no match, and the sheet clears, showing me the most perfect body. Dammit, the daylight makes her even more fucking irresistible. "Jase." She sounds breathless, caught off guard.

Instantly, I'm fucking hard. I growl and her eyes widen, fear and fucking arousal eating her alive. "You're so bad for me. I won't be able to think straight today until I see you again. You're going to make me crazy, Kayla."

She blinks a few times, biting her lip. "Same. I don't know what I'm doing, even sitting here in front of you, but I don't want to be anywhere else."

"Damn right." I bend and grab her ankle, lazily pulling her to me as she slides onto her back.

"Jase, Sadie and Kate are right outside the door."

Kayla blushes as I stand over her, watching her under me like a mirage. This woman isn't real; there's no possible way. "If you are really quiet, I can make it good for you, leave you waiting for me to come to you again."

With a few moments of trepidation, she finally concedes. "Please."

And I do as promised, leaving us both wanting more. And if I don't get back to her soon, I may combust. She falls asleep instantly after our round of lazy fucking, and I leave her with a kiss on her forehead and a note on a magazine I find in one of her unpacked boxes.

§

"Daddy! Good morning!" Avery's voice is welcomed. I hate whole weekends away from her. She's my best friend, and I don't like not being with her whenever I can. But she loves weekends with her grandma, and my mother would have my head if I didn't let her have her.

"Morning, angel. You being good for Nana?" I ask, turning down Harlen's street.

"Sure am! I even woke up early to help her cook breakfast."

I feel guilty, suddenly, knowing I was with a woman who wasn't her mother and missing out on calling her, regardless whether if I knew she was awake or not.

"You could've called me." I pull up behind Harlen, who is cleaning his bike. He gives me a chin lift and gets back to it, while I finish up my call.

"I forgot. I was too excited. Nana made waffles, and I wanted to help!" She's cheerful and carefree, and it lessens the guilt.

"I love her waffles. That was my favorite growing up."

"That's what Nana said. I guess we are just the same, Daddy."

"I guess so, love bug. Well hey, listen, I can't wait to see you tomorrow afternoon, but you make sure to call me in the morning, and don't give Nana any hassle, okay?"

I hear her huff, and I swear I won't survive her. Sassy and undoubtedly gonna be the death of me. "I know, Daddy. You tell me that all the time."

"Don't be sassy. Now go help your grandma around the house and call me tomorrow. I love you."

"Love you too." We end the call and I take a deep breath, because I know what's waiting when I face Harlen.

As I shut the door to my truck, he starts in on me instantly. "Well, well, what an ugly fucker on his walk of shame."

"Piss off, Harlen."

"Yeah, lay off him, baby." Harmony comes out with some drinks for us. I give her a kiss on the cheek and Harlen a fist bump.

"So, do you like her?" Harmony doesn't waste any time.

"I can't give him shit, but you can ask him twenty-one questions? I see how it is, babe."

"Exactly, and don't forget it." She gives me a wink, knowing she is always going to be Harlen's pain in the ass. What I wouldn't give to make Kayla *my* pain in the ass.

"She's something, all right." I rub at the back of my neck.

"My dad says it's *the boom*."

"Explain that to me. You're always saying that," I remark, grabbing one of the boxes with a piece of furniture inside from Harlen's truck next to his bike.

"My dad had it the day he saw my mom, said he felt this weird pull toward her, and instantly, without so much as a few words, he knew he wanted her in his life, in his home, and most definitely in his bed. All my uncles say this too. I thought they were all freaking mental until I met Harlen. I got that exact feeling when I met him." She blushes, and you would think this was the first time they met when they share a look and he grabs her wrist to pull her to him.

"Damn right. Now, don't *you* forget that shit, baby." Grabbing her ass, he lays a long, wet kiss on her, his free hand grabbing her jaw and holding her where he wants her.

"All right, savages, break it up. We have work to do."

They pull away, and Harmony places her hands on her hips knowingly. "You seeing her again tonight?"

"Yeah, I am. I'm going to take her to the lake up by my cabin. Let her see real Tennessee beauty." I rip open the box, getting to work on finishing fast so I can get to her sooner.

"Oh boy, this is going to be fun." She rubs her hands together, and I just shake her off.

I suddenly don't want to talk about how I feel about

Kayla, because I'm still working it out in my head. That, and if I'm being honest, I don't want to share one detail about my girl. Because she's mine. All mine.

Chapter 7

KAYLA

"HOLY HELL! THAT IS HOT! I HAVE NEVER HAD A ONE-NIGHT STAND LIKE that," Kate hollers, slamming her hand down on my kitchen counter as we sip coffee. I explained in vague detail what happened between Jase and me last night, and she and Sadie hung on every word.

"You're telling me. It was a first everything for me, and I still can't believe I did it."

Sadie hasn't said much. She just keeps eyeing me with this knowing smirk.

"What?" I giggle, wanting to know why she's looking at me like she heard a secret about me that I haven't.

"You are in trouble." Her sweet southern drawl comes out.

"And how is that?"

"I married Ben just three weeks after meeting him. I knew by day three of hanging out with him that I loved him. The Ben Cooper effect is what I call it—well, Ben's smart butt is the one who says it."

I chuckle. She never curses because of her hardcore Christian faith. How she married the bad boy rock star still shocks me.

"I'm not marrying Jase. I don't even know his last name," I say matter-of-factly, picking up a grape and eating it. I feel my body ache with the sudden movement, my core tightening. I can still feel him. He never stopped touching me, and he only did when I begged him to, because my body couldn't handle it.

I feel alive and aware of myself, and it's a surreal, bittersweet type of feeling. I feel less empty inside than I did yesterday morning. Tennessee is already bringing me that change I so badly needed. I woke up for once not thinking about how I was going to stomach the day and make it through without hurting. I woke up feeling renewed and profound, and I'm finally living on the edge of excitement for whatever comes next. The shadows of my sadness are becoming less painful.

"You say that now, but we'll see where y'all end up," Sadie adds, taking one last sip of her coffee.

I roll my eyes, and Kate steers the conversation elsewhere. "Well, kid, we have to head back home."

I have dreaded their goodbye, knowing I will now be by myself on this new journey. "You can just stay with me, and I won't tell anyone where you are."

"Yeah, right. Ben would send Nick to come and round us up." Kate blushes when she mentions Nick, but I bite my tongue. She may be with Eric, but she loves Nick, and one day, she will realize it and leave her turbulent relationship with Eric and dive in heart-first with Nick.

"True that. Ben can't go more then two days without

me being in his bed. Loses his darn mind."

"Fine, but promise you guys will come visit me, bring me little pieces of home." My heart grips tight for a second as I realize I'm not in Portland anymore, and my parents home is not just emotionally distant; it's now physically far away.

"Don't look so sad, little bug. We will FaceTime every day. Now, you put your chin up—and those tits—because you have a hot date tonight, and you are going to call and tell me all about it!" Kate pulls me in with her hand on the back of my neck, bringing our foreheads together. "They are here, and that is the realest, most important thing." She drops the humor and brings her hand to my heart for a private moment. "That's your home; that is where they will always be." I feel the tears start to come, and I see hers too. We've been inseparable since we were little, and now I'm suddenly aware of how much I'm going to miss her. "You got this, kiddo. Now go and have a night you won't regret." Giving me a kiss on the cheek, we share soft goodbyes and prolonged hugs before I send them both on their way.

Back inside, I take a moment to look around my new home, to gather my thoughts. Just when I feel more tears coming, my phone in my back pocket distracts me. Thinking it's Kate texting me to tell me to stop crying, because she knows me too well, my stomach flips when I see Jase's name.

Jase: I programmed myself in your phone. I can't stop thinking about us and what last night was. You are fucking eating me alive right now, Kayla. I'm drowning in you. The ball is in your court.

I smile, a small tug of my lips, as I wipe away my last few tears.

Me: Speak for yourself. You started this.

I head toward my room, deciding I better finish the last of the unboxing so I can be ready for school next week and not be completely cluttered with too much to do.

Jase: Nope. Baby, that shit was all you. I didn't stand a chance when you looked at me like you did.

Me: Well, I didn't stand a chance when you touched me the way you did. I guess we are both to blame.

Jase: I guess so.

He responds again, instantly.

Jase: Is this the part where we play twenty-one questions? I think that's how people are doing the dating thing these days. That, or dating app questionnaires.

I chuckle.

Me: No, we don't have to force it. Just like we didn't have to force last night. How about we just talk like we already know each other? What are you up to?

And just like that, we text on and off for a few hours, and not one moment of awkward radio silence happens.

§

I shaved every part of my body as if I were skinning a

wildebeest. I went over every spot until I was sure every speck of hair was gone. I changed a total of five times, and I have gone back and forth from putting my hair in a curly ponytail and down in loose curls enough times to run out of fingers to count on.

My makeup is light. A soft shimmer on my eyes with winged liner and mascara, and set with some gold highlight and bronzed cheeks. I finally decide to leave my hair down and settle on a pair of distressed tight-fitted jeans and a white silk top, a black bralette playing peekaboo out the top. I throw on some black over-the-knee boots and a black leather jacket. My stomach is a ball of nerves, but at least I'm content with what I see in the mirror for the final look.

"Here we go," I whisper to myself just as the doorbell goes off. Grabbing my clutch off my dresser and spritzing myself with some fancy perfume, I hurry along to the door, eager to see him again. And just like I knew he would, he looks irresistible. His hair is styled in a messy crew cut, and his blue jeans and dark grey long-sleeved Henley fit him like a dream.

"Am I gonna lose my breath every damn time I see you?" he asks, pulling me into his body, his arm banding tight around my lower back. His other hand grips my chin and brings me in for a kiss. I go weak, never experiencing such fire and passion with another soul like I have with this handsome, familiar stranger.

"Are you always going to make me breathless with your kisses?" I whisper when we part, his breath warm against my face, the strong scent of mint and him filling my lungs.

"If you let me."

I push back a little and give him a teasing shoulder lift, my face pinching in amusement. "Hm, maybe. We will see how you do tonight."

"Sassy. So damn sassy." He shakes his head and helps me lock the door before taking me to his truck.

"Have you and Kate always been close?" he asks, the sound of country music playing in the background.

"Yeah, we were best friends growing up, not just because we were family, but because I always wanted to be her. I thought the sun rose and set in her ass." I chuckle, and he lets out a throaty laugh that causes me to shiver. Holy hell, that sounded like thick, non-watered-down whiskey.

"She seems like a good time. Sadie doesn't seem like the first candidate to be best friends with her."

"Oh, trust me, it's like the start of a really bad joke. A Christian walks into a Kate Beckett...." I trail off, and he laughs again. I blush when he tightens his hand on my thigh and gives me a compliment.

"Sassy, funny, beautiful, sexy—insatiable. I'm in more trouble than I thought." Shooting me a wink, I bite my lip, trying to calm the tight coil in my stomach.

"It's a God-given gift to be this cool, I guess." I shrug. "Now, what about you and Harlen? How did you two end up being friends?"

"We grew up together. He had a rough go at life, and I was there through it all. We may seem like opposites, but that's my buddy and I wouldn't have it any other way."

"Opposites attract in all things, they say. So your daughter, is she with her mom?" I decide to go for it, rip the Band-Aid off.

"No, she's with my mother for the weekend. My wife passed away a few years ago."

"Oh, Jase." I should slap a hand over my mouth. I should know better, seeing as I'm usually the one on the other end having to awkwardly answer a similar question. "I'm so sorry."

"Don't be sorry. You didn't know."

I recall saying that to him nearly twenty-four hours ago. "What do you do for work?" I drop the heavy and hope this is a much safer question to help relieve the awkwardness around us. Death is never anything but heavy.

"I'm a architect for homes, condos, apartments, sometimes even office buildings." We start slowing down on the highway as he pulls off onto a dirt road.

"That sounds incredible. I can barely color between the lines, so kudos to you for being talented enough to design things," I tell him, and he laughs as we drive deeper into the dark woods, trees thick around us. "I knew it was too good to be true. This isn't the part where Prince Charming turns out to be a serial killer, is it?" I tease... slightly. I realize I'm in the car with a man I barely know, no matter how much my heart tells me otherwise.

"Only if you run." My head whips and my jaw drops as my eyes land on him. He squeezes my thigh again. "I'm kidding, Kayla. Calm down, baby. You are going to love it. I'm about to show you the real perks of living in Tennessee.

"Is it a male strip club? Like those *Magic Mike* guys?" I tease, and I watch his jaw tic.

51

"Cute. Nice try smartass. No. I guess I will add smartass to your list."

Leaning in to soothe his bruised ego, I kiss his cheek. "If it makes you feel better, Jase, I would only want to be your smartass," I whisper.

"That's a dangerous promise," he growls.

"Good. Because you make me feel dangerous." With that, we share body heat and the car fills with desire.

"We're here." He breaks the silence, and I finally take my eyes off him. Looking out the windshield, I see the glistening water.

"Oh my gosh, that's beautiful." At some point in my admiration, Jase climbed out and opened my door. I take his hand, and he leads me out, grabbing a cooler and a blanket from the back of his truck.

"A picnic on the lake? And I thought all those southern love stories were all just made up."

"Those were always false representations of men like me." He takes the lead as I peer up at him.

"How so?"

"Because those men didn't know how to really lay down a lady like I can."

Holy smokes, this man isn't real. I'm about to melt like putty in his hand on a summer day. "Cocky."

"You would know. Very cocky."

I gently nudge my shoulder into him, and we share a laugh. Walking us to the edge of the water, I watch, mesmerized, as he sets up a late-night picnic equipped with two lanterns. I have never had anyone do something so kind for me. This man is really the ultimate, a jack-of-all-trades, a well-rounded, sexy, and generous man.

"It ain't much, but this view is the best part." He takes a seat and holds out his hand to me. "Come here, beautiful." He brings me between his legs, and I snuggle in close. I feel young again, as if this were my first date.

"I used to come out here a lot when I was younger. My dad and I fished all the time."

"I'll be honest. I've never fished in my entire life."

His hand has found its way onto my stomach under the silk fabric where he rubs soft circles. "I can teach you. It's surprisingly calming."

"I will take you up on that."

Giving me a soft kiss to my temple, he opens the cooler and pulls out some drinks and fruit. We spend some time eating in the quiet night, no words being shared just yet. Instead, we enjoy the comfortable silence. He made some delicious chicken we both devoured. My eyes shut and my head rolls back onto his shoulder, the sudden urge to relax into him hitting me.

I hear it then, a sound I know all too well and once loved but now despise, because it holds all the painful memories that haunt me. I hear a sound of thunder, and instantly, I go numb. Please don't let this happen now.

Chapter 8

JASE

A BOLT OF LIGHTENING LIGHTS UP THE SKY, FOLLOWED CLOSELY BY A crack of thunder, and I feel Kayla go tense in my arms, her body nearly turning to brick. "Hey, it's all right. Just a little lightening. We may get some rain. I've got you though, beautiful." Suddenly, she wiggles her way from between my legs and arms and stands abruptly. Panic is all over her face, and her neck has gone beet red. "Kayla, what's wrong?" I stand quickly and grab her face. A cool breeze hits us, and I see a drop of rain land on her cheek. Her eyes begin to well with tears as her hair blows in the rainy wind, and immediately, something changes in her. Fear. She's afraid, and I worry it was me who did something wrong.

She doesn't answer. Instead, she goes more and more into her own head, and I panic. "Baby, what the hell is going on?" And as if the clouds heard me and felt my worry, they open up and we drown in rain, as it comes down harsh and heavy. "Fuck, come on. Let's get out of here." I grab her hand and leave everything behind. I will come back for it later. Pulling her and setting her cemented feet into motion, she follows me. I swing open her door and help her in before hurrying to my side. Once there, I start up my truck, putting it in Reverse, but I stop at the sound of shrill panic.

"No! Don't we can't drive!"

"What?" I turn to her, completely shell-shocked. I have no damn idea what's going on, but it sure as hell is a mind trip.

"We can't drive. Can we wait in the truck until the rain passes?"

Looking at her, her small hands are curled into even tighter fists, the skin stretching so tight they've gone pale. Her eyes are squeezed shut, and I'm sure that's not rain running down her cheeks, but tears. I know, because they are accompanied by whimpers.

I look around for a second, taking in my surroundings and making sure this isn't just a dream. Turning my eyes back to her, I shake my head, even though she can't see me. "We can't sit in the truck. This will last hours. The forecast said today we could expect showers late this evening and they would last all night. We will get cold, and I can't leave the truck running, babe. I can get us home. Just—"

"No, Jase! We can't!" She snaps her eyes open, landing on me.

I grow irritated, but seeing how upset she is, I try to keep my cool. "Why? What in the world is going on, Kayla?"

She shakes her head, mumbling over and over the

words "I can't. I can't."

Doing my best not to lose my temper with her non answer, I grip the steering wheel a couple times and release a deep breath. "Fine. I have a cabin less than half a mile away. Can I at least drive us there?"

Kayla hesitates, looking from me to the windshield, where the rain pelts my truck. She gulps deep then nods slowly. "Just, please, drive slow."

"Yeah, okay," I respond, putting my car in drive.

I get us there in less than three minutes. I climb out and help her down, the rain once again blasting and drenching us through completely. Getting us inside as fast as possible, I try to flip on the lights, but they aren't working, and I'm sure its due to the storm tonight and the other ones we've had between Avery's and my last visit here. I use the moonlight to help guide me around the familiar space, and I take the wood from our last time here and toss it in the fireplace. Lighting a few matches, I get the fire going, giving the living area a soft amber glow.

I stand back, keeping my hands on my hips and my head dropped low as I watch the flames, and shake my head slowly. What in the actual hell is going on with her right now?

"I—I'm so sorry, Jase. I'm j-j-just a little a-a-afraid of the rain," she stutters through tears and body chills from the chill.

Turning then, I decide I better just come out and ask. "You gotta give me an explanation for whatever that was, Kayla." She nods, dropping her head in embarrassment. It breaks my heart to see her so torn up and ashamed. This really must mean something to her, whatever it is inside her that has her so damn afraid.

I step up to her without words and begin to remove her clothes. She doesn't question me or try to stop me, still too lost in her own mind to even do so. Feeling like ice, she is frozen to the bone, and I know it's not just the rain that caused it.

Once she is bare to me, I take her clothes and hang them in the bathroom above the tub, then remove mine and do the same. Lucky for me, I have my cabin stocked with everything that it needs in case this happens, including a wireless space heater you crank up to turn on. Giving it a few long and hard spins, it kicks on, and I put it close to the clothes I just rung out and hung, hoping it will dry them out.

Coming back out, I'm surprised to see she has wrapped herself in a blanket and planted herself on the rug in front of the fire. Hearing me enter the room, she looks up to me with a soft smile that doesn't reach her eyes.

I huff, feeling like a total jackass. I snipped at her a couple times, and I must have been clueless to see this is something serious and meaningful to her. Whatever her fear is, it's significant, and I should have realized that and respected it before snapping.

"Can you let me in?" Unashamed of my nakedness, I stand above her as she nods, opening the blanket wrapped around her. Her knees are touching and pressed up against her chest as I move myself to place my legs on each side of her hips. Maneuvering her, I grab her ankles and place her feet behind me. Pulling her up and onto my lap so she is straddling me, her chest bare against mine, our body heat warms us up and brings us a connection I feel we will need for this conversation. "Let me in here, baby." I lean down and kiss above her perfect breast. "And here." I bring my lips to her temple. Her green eyes lock on mine, and I see a war wage deep inside her. "You can trust me. I will hold your secrets tight and forever."

She exhales a soft breath. "That's how they passed. My parents died from a car accident in the rain."

Shit. The poor girl hasn't healed at all. No, she is still as broken as the day it happened, and I can tell that all by that solemn look and through my connection with her.

"Release that pain, baby. It's going to suffocate you if you don't." I kiss the top of her shoulder over and over again, her tears sounding like the anthem of her broken heart.

"I lost them in the rain. They were my soul, Jase. My everything. And in a blink, they were gone."

"I know. I know that feeling all too well. But you are never going to heal the pain if you don't feel it first, baby. It's okay to feel it."

"If I feel it, I'm scared it will kill me. It will just burn every part of me until I'm nothing but ashes."

"From the rubble, the ashes will rise, and they will fly in the passing wind," I whisper against her neck, my heart held tightly in a grip by her pain. I know the pain of loss, and I know living in that pain can destroy you. But I also know there is something worth living and overcoming for, and I see it in my daughter's eyes every damn day. I see it in Kayla's eyes right here and right now.

"I used to dance with my father in the rain, all the time. We laughed so hard. My mom would watch us from the porch. She hated to get her hair wet, because it would curl into an untamed mess." She giggles through a sniffle, her eyes dancing in the flicks of light from the fire, and it's like she's reliving those moments as we sit here. "Those moments happened so often it became our favorite thing to do; it became my best memory. And now, whenever rain comes, so do the reminders that they are gone. The one thing we loved the most took away what I loved the most." I wipe away her tears, watching her closely, listening to every word. "I know it sounds so childish and melodramatic. But it's the truth." She shrugs and drops her eyes to her hands on my chest, but I don't let her think for one second that it is anything but painful reality.

"It's not. It's raw and real. It's your heartbreak, baby, and you have every right to hold on to it. But you can't let it take away everything. You have to remember the good that came with the rain. Maybe..." I pause, pulling her in tighter, wanting her close. "Maybe every time it rains, they are there reminding you of all the great moments you felt closest to them. Maybe they are urging you to let go and dance in the rain again."

"Jase," she breaths.

"When I lost Lainey to cancer, I saw her in my daughter every day. I saw the same thing you saw in the rain. I saw pain and reminders of what I lost, but after I realized I had something so much more in my daughter, I stopped looking at her with pain, but with a life of memories and love. I knew I had something to always keep me close to Lainey. Avery became the only thing that kept me alive."

"You seem like an incredible father, and I'm so sorry you lost your true love. I couldn't imagine." She turns the comfort on me.

"It was unimaginable, but Avery got me through it. She gave me purpose, and I knew with time my heart would heal its own wound."

"Did it? Is it healed all the way yet?" she questions.

I take a deep breath and search her eyes, my hands tightening on her back. "Not until I met you," I choke out, unable to believe I'm actually admitting this to her.

"I came here, because I was running from something. But then I met you, and I knew I wasn't running. I was chasing. I was searching for *you*."

I kiss her then, bringing her soft, plump lips, swollen from her tears and fresh with her confession, to mine and I claim her. I take what I know was made to be mine. I loved my wife and I always will, but I know Kayla was sent to me from Lainey. My wife sent me a fucking angel.

And the way I know this? Because no one could take my heart in their hands in one damn day. No one. But someone who was made for you could have the power to fucking do it. And here Kayla sits, in my lap and inside my heart, so damn deep I couldn't break the connection if I tried.

"I want you. Show me how we heal each other," she whispers into the cabin, as my lips descend on her neck, leaving love bites anywhere I can.

I growl, kissing my way back to her mouth, our tongues fighting for dominance. She tastes so damn good, like new beginnings and painless tomorrows. I will make sure I do whatever I can to keep Kayla in my life. Keep her as mine and learn who she is. I will fall in love first and discover everything about her as we build a life. We are doing this all backwards, but my head and heart have never been more in sync and sure of what tomorrow is going to bring.

Gripping her hips, I lift her and line her up with my cock. Biting at her bottom lip, I slowly bring her down, our breaths catching as our lips part. We watch each other, our brows drawn in euphoric pain. Fuck, she feels like a dream.

"Hold on, baby." I slow her hips as she tries to lift up again, attempting to take the reins on her first time riding my cock. "If we go too fast, I won't be able to make this last. You're killing me." Nodding, her eyes hazy and lost in lust, she bites her lip, her slowly drying hair clinging to the sides of her neck. "You have to let me guide you. I don't want this to hurt you, sweet girl." I start to lift her up and down slowly, watching her mouth fall open, her jaw hanging in a sexy way. I know I'm too big and this is still hurting her, but she likes it and, God knows, so do I. I will die a happy man if I can put that look on her face every night.

"Mmmm. Baby, just like that. Does it feel good? You like slow, sweet?" My voice is low. I'm a monster in a cage, waiting for its captor to let him free.

"It hurts a little. A little softer." Her eyes dance over my face.

"Relax and open up for me, baby. I can't stop the pain if you don't relax. Let me take control." She nods as I feel her legs loosen a little, and my cock finishes sliding in the last few inches. We both gasp. "You're perfect, Kayla. I won't be able to let you run from me."

"Oh!" she gasps. I hit her deep, right against that sweet spot. "I don't want to run."

Grabbing her throat softly yet with firm intention, I watch as her breath deepens and her eyes fall on mine. "You are going to give me a child, a life, a home, aren't you, sweet thing?" I start to pick up the pace now that she has grown accustomed to my girth.

"You're that sure of me?"

"I'm that sure. In fact, I look forward to the day you stop taking your pill. The day you are under my roof as mine and I come home to claim this sweet pussy you give me every night. I will fuck you so deep and good that you'll be pregnant before you even beg for mercy. I'm going to take whatever is mine and whatever you give me. Aren't I, baby?"

"I think this is lust speaking." She lets out a loud moan as I thrust into her for testing me.

"Whatever helps you sleep at night, sweetheart, but accept what is."

"And what's that?" She leans in and kisses my neck, a siren in sheep's clothing this little one is.

"Oh, baby," I moan. "Fuck, I'm falling in love with you." I don't give her a chance to speak. Instead, I flip her under me and let the flames burn alongside our lovemaking as I drive my point home, making her come at the same time I do, our names a choked scream on each other's dry lips.

Chapter 9

KAYLA

I FELL ASLEEP AFTER JASE CONFESSED HIS STRONG FEELINGS FOR ME, THE same ones building inside me. I wanted to tell him I'm feeling the same way, but he made love to me until my eyes closed and I didn't even have a chance. I hear ringing in the background of my dream state, and it pulls me into consciousness.

"Hello," Jase answers his cell, fresh from sleep as well. I'm sprawled out on his chest and looking up at him. "Fuck, Mom, is she okay? I'm on my way. I will be right there!"

Suddenly, I jump up and he follows, hurrying toward the bathroom where he put our clothes.

"Jase, what's going on? Is it Avery?" I ask, panicked, following him so I can get dressed.

"She fell and hit her head. They had to give her stitches. She's at the hospital, and I have to get to her," he explains, and I drop the blanket and grab my nearly dry clothes, dressing quickly. "It's still raining out, so throw some more wood on the fire and I'll come back and get you once I find out if she's okay." He's a wreck, his face contorted in pure pain and near hysteria.

"No, I'm going with you."

He stops once his shoes are on and gives me a look of uncertainty. "But the rain, baby." He grabs my face, and I can tell he is trying to go slow and be in the moment with me, yet still trying to get out the door.

"I don't care. I'm worried for her too, and I'm not going to make you go alone. Besides," I mimic him, grabbing his face in my hands, "I'm not scared of the rain so much anymore." I smile and give him a brisk kiss, turning to head for the door. He doesn't move until I put him in place. "Dump some water on the fire and let's go, baby!" That sets him into motion, and within five minutes, we are in his truck and leaving the way we came.

I'm a mess, my insides torn up with nausea, but I hide it. I may be convinced I will one day not fear the rain, but that comes with time. I'm nowhere near fearless of the slippery roads and the heavy rainfall, but I care more about him and Avery. I want to be here for him and make sure she is okay. I don't even know her, yet I'm more worried for her than I am my own mental health.

"You didn't have to do this, Kayla. I really can't thank you enough." He breaks the silence, his eyes never leaving the road as his jaw tics. I appreciate his safety precautions for me, not speeding, even though I know he's dying to.

"I wouldn't want to be anywhere else. I just want to get you to Avery."

He smiles this time, and comfort washes over both of us. "Thank you."

We stay silent, and within twenty minutes, we are screeching to a halt at the ER entrance. I don't wait for him to open my door; I'm out and right beside him as we run through the sliding doors.

"Avery Riding, my daughter was just brought here. Which room is she?" he asks frantically.

"She is in room 104, but it is family only, sir."

"That's fine. This is my wife," he lies, but the title still makes my stomach flip. A good kind of flip. She smiles and nods, pointing us in the right direction, and Jase takes my hand, walking us briskly down the hall. Coming into the room, I see who I believe is his mother holding a sleeping Avery's hand in hers. His daughter lies in the bed with a bandage on her right temple.

"Mom, what the hell happened?" he questions, keeping his voice low and letting me go while hurrying to Avery's side. I watch him cling to her hand, kissing it over and over again, his eyes welling with tears. It's a beautiful, raw moment, and once again, it shows me a different side of Jase. One that I fall for. I have seen many sides of him in just twenty-four hours, and they are all beautiful.

"I put her to bed upstairs then went back down to clean up our mess and watch some TV, when suddenly I heard a bang. I ran up and saw she tripped and hit her head on the edge of the desk by the bedroom door. I think she was trying to go to the bathroom and was a little out of it and tripped over the rug." His mom finally looks at me where I stand, still in the doorway, not wanting to interrupt their private family moment. She gives me a genuine smile that reaches her eyes, and I immediately don't feel as nervous. I'm sure she is curious who this random woman is with her son in her granddaughter's hospital room.

"Shit, Mom, sorry. This is my girlfriend, Kayla." Girlfriend? Another little flip in my stomach. I'm his girlfriend?

"Watch your mouth around the sweet girl. Kayla, nice to meet you. I'm Paula." She stands and heads toward me, and I mentally kick myself into gear. I meet her at the front of the bed and reach out to shake her hand. She waves me off and pulls me in for a tight, welcoming hug. Jase looks at us briefly, giving a soft smile, but his eyes go back to Avery just as quickly.

"It's so nice to meet you, ma'am."

We separate and she chuckles, tucking my hair behind my ear. "Please don't call me ma'am. I already feel old with all my gray hairs. Please, call me Paula, or Ma, whichever you like, sweetie."

"I can do that."

"Excuse me, can I speak to the legal guardian outside?" the doctor interrupts, and Jase turns to face him.

"Uh, yeah, sure thing." He stands eagerly, and Paula follows him out to the hall, leaving me with Avery.

I look over her sleeping face, and I see so much of Jase in her. Going to take a seat next to her, I set my bag down on the floor, and when I turn back to face her, her eyes are now open and on me. "Oh, um... hi, sweetheart. I didn't hear you wake up," I say stupidly, mentally kicking myself for being so nervous around a five-year-old.

She gives me a soft smile. "It's okay. Who are you? Are you a nurse lady?"

I chuckle, leaning closer. "No, I'm actually your dad's

g— friend, Kayla. I was with him when we got the call about your head. Are you feeling all right?" I leave out the girlfriend part and focus on comforting her until her dad gets back. I reach forward and move her hair from the side of her face that isn't hurt, and she suddenly grabs my hand. Little tears fill her eyes, and I worry it's because of me. "Sweetheart, don't cry. It's okay."

"No, I don't like hospitals. They make my daddy really sad. I don't like it here."

"I know. I'm sorry. I'm not a fan of them either, so what do you say we play a game?" I think of something quick, something to distract her and put her at ease.

"Mm-kay." Her voice is a low excited whisper, and it steals my heart. What a precious little thing.

"Okay, so I'm thinking of an animal, my favorite one, and if you can guess what it is, I will give you a dollar," I tell her. She smiles and perks up suddenly, and my throat clogs with emotion when she wraps her tiny little hand around mine. I look from her to my hand then back again, and she wears a beautiful smile, the same one as her father's. I cough through the emotions. "Okay, go ahead and take a guess."

"Okay, I think it's a…" She pauses and thinks long and hard. I go with the obvious in my mind, which is a dog, because who doesn't love dogs?

"I think it's a puppy!" I drop my jaw in mock surprise.

"You are one clever little girl. You won! Okay, now you think of one, and the same goes if I lose. You get a dollar."

"Oh, I like this game." I squeeze her hand and watch her close her eyes, thinking of the best answer. "Okay, ready. You go."

"Hmm, I'm thinking it's probably a... a cat!"

"Ew, no! I love puppies too!"

"Well dang, looks like you are the best at this game. That's two bucks!"

She giggles, and I see her forget where she is at the moment. I keep it up, and we share a few more laughs, and of course I let her win each time.

"Hey, angel." Jase and Paula return, and they both watch us, soft smiles on their faces.

"Hey, Daddy!" she says excitedly, completely unfazed by her injury.

"What am I going to do with you? You about gave me a heart attack," he says, coming to her side and bringing her little hand to his heart.

"Daddy, you say that about everything I do. You're such a weirdo." We all laugh, and I get what he means; she is a handful, and the cutest one there is. Jase will need a cardiologist by forty at this rate.

"Now you know why. You did this at grandma's house."

She shrugs him off. Looking up at me, she gives me a toothy smile. "So, Daddy, is Kayla your girlfriend?"

My jaw drops, and Paula snorts, covering her mouth to mask it.

"Why would you ask that, little one?" He sits down in the chair next to her bed and looks at her then to me, and I see amusement in his eyes, unlike what's in mine. I'm mortified. I don't want to tell her anything that will upset her. I can't imagine she would be ready to share her father with anyone, especially someone she just met.

"Because you need one. Then you can quit telling me what to do all the time. You know, pick on someone your own size."

Jase shakes his head, and we all share laughs as we watch her. "No more TV for you, pipsqueak. Well, I would like her to be my girlfriend, but I may need some help convincing her. You think you're up for the challenge?"

"Jase!" I shake my head. He is incorrigible and apparently mentally unstable.

"Please, Kayla! I like you a lot, and I want Daddy to have more friends! Especially girls, because he's bad at doing hair and yours is so pretty. You can maybe do mine sometime!" She claps, and just like that, she steals my heart after only a short time of knowing her. I think it must be a Riding thing, because she is just like her handsome father.

"As long as you and I get to have girls' nights," I bargain, and her eyes light up.

"Yay! Daddy, I have a new friend, and you have a girlfriend! But no kissing in front of me. That's how you get germs."

Jase looks guilty, and I give him a head tilt, imploring with a look.

"I told her kissing gives you germs, so she shouldn't kiss any boys. I got desperate; I don't have the stomach or blood pressure to deal with her dating."

"Jase Riding, you are something else. She's *five*."

"Gotta teach 'em young. And right back at you, baby."

Shaking my head at him, I look back to Avery's little dimpled smile and I ponder the thought for extra effect. She waits excitedly and barely able to contain herself, before I speak. "I think I like your daddy a lot. How about I give him a chance?"

"Yes! Oh, yay! Nana, did you hear that! Now my hair wont look like such a mess all the time."

I peek a look at Paula and she is smiling adoringly at Avery and I sneak a look to Jase. He watches me, shaking his head and softly asking, "who are you."

I shrug and recite the same remark, because his guess is just as good as mine.

But what I do know. Is who he is, is exactly where I want to be and who I want to be with. I want to chase this new beginning and ride the wave of instant connection. I don't want to run from my past now, I want to heal and I know indefinitely that my parents placed Jase in my life, just when I needed him and he needed me. We are a match made to last, a touch of faith built in the hands of the loved ones we lost.

I love Jase and it has only been one day. What in the hell would a lifetime with him be like?

Until Jase Riding and sweet little Avery, I didn't know what feeling again would be like. And little did I know, it was everything all at once. Powerful, beautiful, reckless, and healing. He let me in his life, and I let him in mine, faster than you could say *"boom."*

Epilogue

JASE

"JASE, STOP, THE GIRLS ARE HOME." KAYLA TRIES TO CRAWL OUT OF BED and away from me.

Not gonna happen on my watch.

"Yeah, and they are still asleep, and I haven't had that tight little pussy in forever," I growl, bringing her under me and climbing between her legs before she can protest again.

"We had sex last night," she says matter-of-factly.

"Yeah, and that's too long. We've been married five years, baby. When you gonna learn that if it ain't daily, it ain't enough. I'm fucking obsessed, and so are you." With that, I line myself up and slide in, the silk on her chest slipping and showing me her tight rosy nipple. I lean down and take it in my mouth, giving it a harsh suck and nip.

"Ah, Jase!"

I hurry and cover her mouth, because I don't plan to stop this train early, and if she wakes Avery and our two-

year-old, Lainey, we won't be able to make love. And I
need to make love to her, because today I know for a
fact my woman is ovulating, and I'm ready for another
baby. A little boy this time. "You gotta keep those moans
quiet, wife. Whisper them in my ear while I make you feel
good."

She nods and I move my hand, bringing it to her thigh
and lifting it higher up my side so I can be all the way
inside her warm pussy.

"I'm on to you. You read my fertility app, didn't you?"
She cries out when I nip her dimpled cheek. I love that
fucking dimple.

"You bet that sweet ass I did. I want more," I growl,
pounding into her, mating with her.

"I know you do, but all you had to do was ask. You
know I can't tell you no." She gives me a sassy little grin,
and it makes my chest puff up.

This woman has never stopped surprising me. In the
six years I have known and loved her, she has never quit
taking my breath away. We are still two people falling
in love, and I don't think we will ever settle down. We
married just two months after meeting, and every day
since, I have learned something new about my amazing
woman. "I know, but sometimes I like to surprise you, like
you surprise me every day." I flip us then and put her on
top of me. "Besides that, I want to watch you be a mom
again. You are such an incredible fucking mother, baby."
Her silk nightie slips from her shoulders and collects at
her waist, exposing her perfect body. Kayla hasn't aged, I
swear.

After she gave me our second daughter, who she named

after the angel who brought us together, I knew I would mate her until she begged me not to anymore. I'll make a damn village with her if she'll let me.

Avery has grown into a young lady, and a beautiful, kind one at that, and it's all because she had a mother like Kayla in her life. After the day we left the hospital with Avery, Kayla never questioned her responsibility and love for our daughter. She's raised her as if she were from her own womb. She lives for our little girls, and what man wouldn't want to see that over and over again?

"And I'm only this good because of the man I raise them with. You are an incredible father, handsome."

I watch, mesmerized, as we flip over and she slowly rides my cock, complimenting me and spoiling me with her words. "Fuck, I'm gonna come. Grab your tits, baby. Let me see you come first."

She follows my orders as we both pick up the pace, matching each other thrust by thrust. "I love you, Jase!"

Shit.

Just like that, I come, losing myself in my love, my life, the perfect fucking ending.

Our breathing is laborious as we stay wrapped in one another for a moment longer. But like every morning, our girls come barreling down the hall.

A knock on the door sounds, and Kayla hurries to fix her silk nightie as I grab my sweatpants off the floor and slide them on. "Mama, Daddy, are you awake?" Avery asks from the other side.

Opening the door, I'm greeted with a wild-haired, sleepy-eyed Lainey holding her big sister's hand. "Morning, beautiful girls." I let them in, and Avery walks straight to Kayla as Lainey reaches her arms for me to pick her up.

Kayla pulls Avery in for a hug and kisses her forehead. "Happy birthday, Avery bug."

Today, Avery turns twelve, and I have been dreading it worse than the birthday the year before. She is growing up too damn fast. I join them back in bed, and Lainey gives her mom a kiss and then snuggles in between Avery and me. I swear if I could be a fly on the wall, I would see the vision of us here as a family and capture that moment in a mental snapshot.

"Thanks, Mama. We still good to go shopping for my new school clothes?"

"You bet, and we will even get you something that will give your dad heart palpitations. Maybe a phone," Kayla whispers conspiratorially.

"Really?" She claps excitedly, and I tighten my grip on Kayla's neck where my arms rest behind all my girls. She giggles and gives me a wink.

"Don't test me, woman."

"Oh hush, you caveman. We are just teasing."

Avery laughs and looks between us both. "I'm glad it isn't just me causing him all the gray hairs."

With that, I stand on the bed, towering over them, before bending and pulling all of my girls in for morning tickles. They all try to escape, but they're no match for me. And just like that, I remember exactly how blessed I am to have met Kayla all those years ago, falling in love with her so fast and recklessly without a care in the world. Saying a quick prayer up to my angel, Lainey, I wrap myself up in the love of my three girls.

Until Kayla Mackey, I was incomplete and looking for the one thing that could give me life again. Someone to ensure my daughter would never go a lifetime without knowing the love of a mother. Kayla was that missing piece we needed, and we chased it faster than you could say *"boom."*

The End.

Now go out there and find yourself that Boom.

ALSO BY CC MONROE

<u>Always and Forever Series</u>
Always the One
Always Us
Forever the One
Forever Us

Steal You: A Standalone Dark Romance

<u>Crossover Series with Aurora Rose Reynolds</u>
Until Kayla
Until Mercy

ACKNOWLEDGMENTS

Aurora. This is a dream. You are the one who introduced me to alphas and this beautiful indie community. You inspired me to start writing again, after I swore I never would after the abuse. You are an incredible human and you inspire me with your words and many other aspects in life. This book is in honor of you and the incredible world you built. I love you bunches, lady. Never forget it!

Toddy, you are my world. My HEA. My BOOM. You saved me from a life so damn dark I didn't think I would make it. That was until you. Forever and always, TJB.

Lashelle. Love you too much.

Kayla. You are my sister wife and other half. I love you. Stay incredible. pretty. My wallet wants to slap you. I love you .

My readers, my honeys. You're my inspiration and I write my books for you. Never forget it. To the ones with a BOOM, hold them tight and roll your eyes often. To the ones searching, he is coming and you better be ready.

ABOUT THE AUTHOR

Author CC Monroe is from the hottest city in the world, Phoenix, Arizona. She spends her days working and her nights with her face in her laptop telling the stories of the voices in her mind. She left Arizona a few years back and now lives in the beautiful snow state of Utah, where she married her true love!

When she isn't writing or working, she is making people laugh with her mad sense of humor and tip of the tongue one liners.

Follow her on Facebook and Instagram